Richard Scarry's
Best Christmas Book Ever!

First published in 1981
This edition published by HarperCollins *Children's Books* in 2014
HarperCollins *Children's Books* is a division of HarperCollins Publishers Ltd,
77-85 Fulham Palace Road, London W6 8JB

1 3 5 7 9 10 8 6 4 2

ISBN:978-0-00-752315-3

© 1981 Richard Scarry Corporation

www.harpercollins.co.uk

Printed and bound in China.

Richard Scarry's
Best Christmas Book Ever!

HarperCollins *Children's Books*

Jingle Bells

J. Pierpont

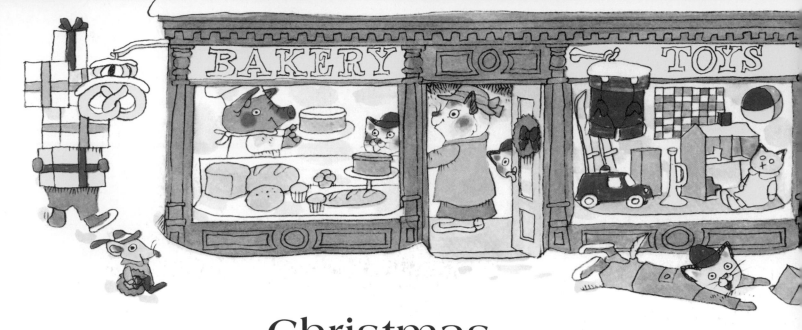

Christmas
is Coming!

Busytown is getting ready for Christmas. The firefighters are stringing lights on the buildings. The stores are crowded with shoppers. Everyone is busy. Look! There's Big Hilda with Huckle Cat and his sister, Sally, in a big sleigh. Lowly Worm is pulling it with his appletractor. Now, where are they going?

They are going to get a Christmas tree!
Farmer Pig has many beautiful pine trees on his farm.
Maybe he will give one to them. When he hears how they
are going to use the tree, Farmer Pig is happy to help.

TIMBER!

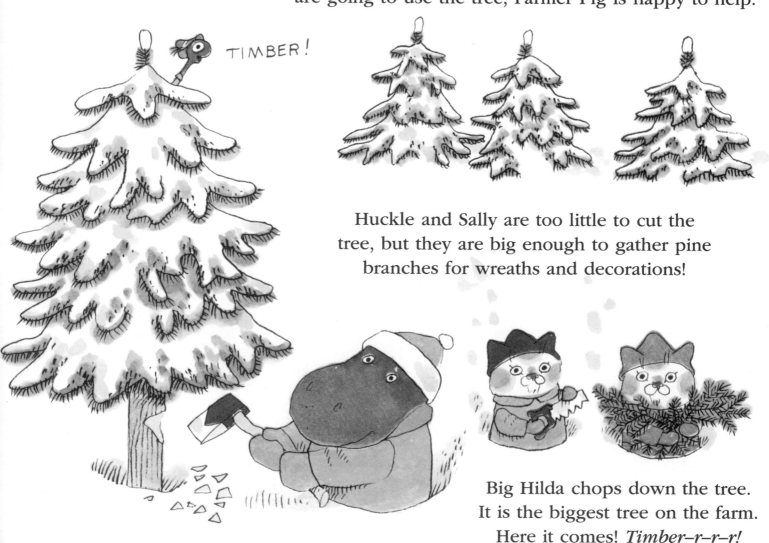

Huckle and Sally are too little to cut the
tree, but they are big enough to gather pine
branches for wreaths and decorations!

Big Hilda chops down the tree.
It is the biggest tree on the farm.
Here it comes! *Timber–r–r!*

They all help to put the tree on the sleigh.
"Come and see the tree when we get it decorated,"
says Huckle. "I'll try," says Farmer Pig,
who is snowed in.

Lowly drives the sleigh back
to town. They put the tree up
in the town square and decorate
it with lights and ornaments.
Lowly puts a star at the top.
Everyone comes to admire the tree
– even Farmer Pig. Now Busytown
is *really* ready for Christmas.

Doctor Bones is Good All Year Round

All year round Doctor Bones is busy calling on his sick patients. Sometimes it is very hard for him to make his house calls. In the winter his car often gets stuck in the snow.

When the streets are icy, he must drive very carefully to avoid an accident. Look out, Doctor Bones! Your car is skidding on the ice!

Sometimes in the spring it rains so hard that the streets become flooded. Then his car stops dead. Surprise, Doctor Bones, that puddle is too deep to drive through!

Often he gets stuck in the mud. It is hard work – and very messy – to push the car out.

But Doctor Bones never gives up. His sick patients appreciate how hard he works for them. "We will remember you at Christmas," they all tell him.

Mrs Cat does not complain about the bumpy ride to the hospital. She is thankful that the good Doctor Bones can take her there.

Look out for that curve, Doctor! Too late! His car goes over the guard rail and falls into the sea. But Captain Pig saves him.

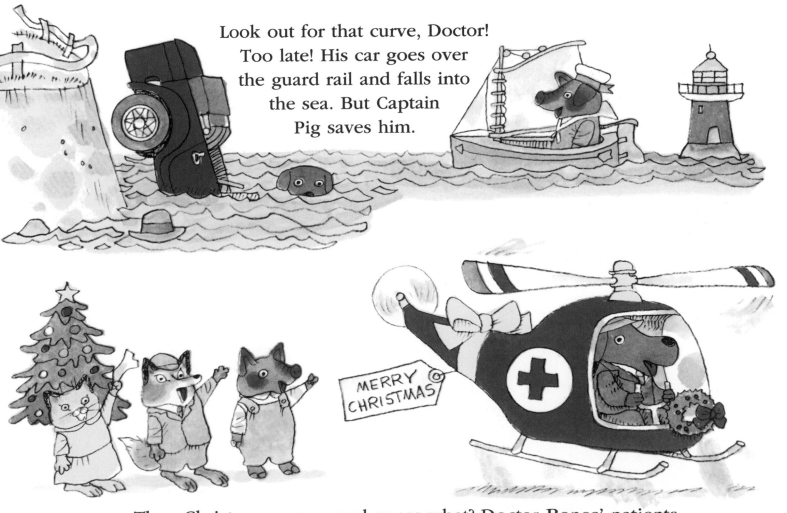

MERRY CHRISTMAS

Then Christmas comes, and guess what? Doctor Bones' patients all remember to remember him. They give him a brand-new helicopter. Now he will have no problem visiting them.
Merry Christmas, Doctor Bones, the Flying Doctor!

Grouchy Mr Gronkle

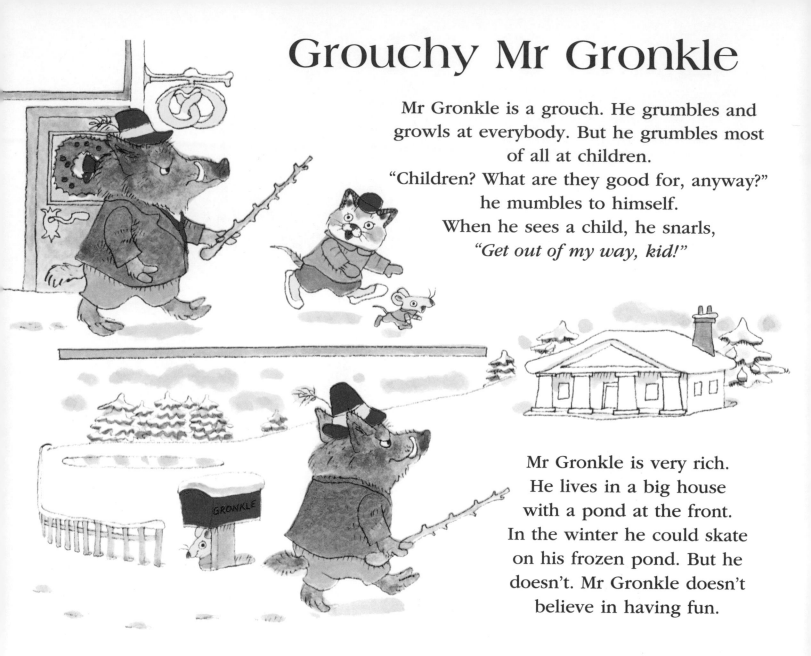

Mr Gronkle is a grouch. He grumbles and
growls at everybody. But he grumbles most
of all at children.
"Children? What are they good for, anyway?"
he mumbles to himself.
When he sees a child, he snarls,
"Get out of my way, kid!"

Mr Gronkle is very rich.
He lives in a big house
with a pond at the front.
In the winter he could skate
on his frozen pond. But he
doesn't. Mr Gronkle doesn't
believe in having fun.

And he doesn't believe in
having friends. He lives alone
in that big old house.
Why, he won't even let someone
come in to help him clean his
house. It looks like a pigsty.

One fine day just before Christmas, Lowly Worm suggests that they all go ice skating on Mr Gronkle's pond.

"We should ask his permission first," says Huckle Cat. "To be sure that it's safe." "Oh, I'm sure Mr Gronkle won't mind," says Lowly.

But Mr Gronkle DOES mind. He is furious. He runs down to the frozen pond swinging his walking stick. He runs onto the ice…

Look out, Lowly!

OOPS!!

Mr Gronkle slips.

CRRAACK! Right through the ice he goes and into the freezing water.

"Help! Save me!" he cries. He tries to climb out, but the ice cracks more. He can't get out by himself. At first the children feel that it serves nasty old Mr Gronkle right. But then they begin to feel sorry for him.

"He'll soon freeze in the cold water," says Huckle. "We must help him."

"Don't leave me here!" shouts Mr Gronkle when he sees the children running off.

But they are not leaving him. They are going to find a ladder.

Huckle puts the ladder on the ice.

Lowly winds himself like a rope around Mr Gronkle's nose.
"What are those terrible children doing?" wonders
Mr Gronkle. Then they all pull on Lowly.

Slowly they pull Mr Gronkle out of the water and on to the ice. "You're the best rope ever, Lowly," says Huckle.

"Now I know what children are good for," says Mr Gronkle. They're good for saving grouchy, grumpy Mr Gronkle."

Mr Gronkle promises to change his nasty ways. He starts by having a wonderful Christmas party for all the children. He has such a good time that he decides to turn his house into a play centre!

Now grouchy, grumpy Mr Gronkle is called cheerful, friendly Mr G. He's always busy seeing that the children have a good time at his house.
Merry Christmas, Mr Gronkle!

Postman Pig and Aunt Kitty

Postman Pig is busier than ever at Christmas time. There are so many Christmas cards and presents to deliver. Today he has a letter for old Aunt Kitty. That pleases him because Aunt Kitty lives alone and has no friends.

Aunt Kitty is pleased to get the letter, too. "Oh, do come in and have a cup of hot chocolate while I read my letter," she says.

Aunt Kitty reads the letter and bursts into tears. "Oh, boo, hoo, hoo!" she cries. "My niece won't be able to visit me at Christmas. I will be all alone." Postman Pig starts to cry, too. *"Boo, hoo, hoo!"*

Going back to the post office, Postman Pig meets Lowly and tells him Aunt Kitty's sad news. They both cry. "We must do something for her," says Lowly.

Then Lowly tells Huckle Cat
about lonely Aunt Kitty.

And Huckle tells his mother.
"Boo, hoo, hoo!" he cries.

Mother Cat tells Ma Pig. "Oh
isn't that a shame!" they say.

Ma Pig tells Sergeant Murphy
Even the brave sergeant cries!
"Boo, hoo, hoo!"

Soon everyone in Busytown hears
the sad story of Aunt Kitty.

And soon everyone is extra busy –
sewing, baking, and making things.

Then, on Christmas morning, who do you think comes
to visit Aunt Kitty? EVERYONE in Busytown! And each
with a wonderful present. Aunt Kitty is so happy to see
that she has so many friends after all.

Trouble at Santa's Workshop

In Santa's workshop there are
hundreds of elves who work, work,
work all day long making toys for
Santa to bring at Christmas.

Some of the elves want to work all night
long, too, but Santa won't let them. "You need a good
night's sleep to work well the next day," he tells them.
And they can't disobey Santa – even if they would
like to – because he locks up all the tools at night.

Then, one morning Santa
discovers that he has lost the
key to his tool cupboard!

Santa and Mrs Claus
look everywhere for the key.
But they can't find it.

"I know!" says Santa. "I'll call my good friend Lowly Worm and ask him to bring me some keys that might fit."

Lowly is happy to help – if he can.

Lowly goes to the locksmith's and gets big keys and little keys, thick keys and thin keys.

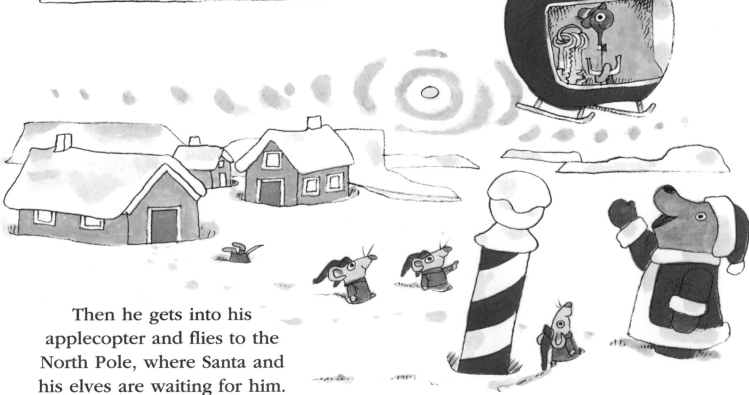

Then he gets into his applecopter and flies to the North Pole, where Santa and his elves are waiting for him.

Santa takes Lowly to the locked tool cupboard door. "One of these keys will surely fit," says Lowly.

He tries one. It doesn't work.

He tries another and another and another. But none of the keys that Lowly has will fit the lock.

"This is terrible!" sighs Lowly. "If I can't open this lock, there will be no toys for Christmas." He puts his eye right up to the keyhole and looks inside. Then suddenly he has an idea!

He takes off his shoe.

Then he takes off his sock.

And he wiggles his bare foot around.

He puts his foot in the keyhole and twists and turns his toe.

Click, goes the lock! Lowly Key smiles. "I opened it!"

The elves rush to get their tools and hurry back to their work benches. There will be toys for Christmas after all. *Hurrah!*

"May I make a toy too before I leave?" Lowly asks Santa. "Please do!" says Santa. "We need all we can make."

Then Santa thanks him for all his help, and Lowly hops into his applecopter and flies safely home.

Maybe one of the toys you get for Christmas will be the very one that Lowly made!

Big Hilda Helps Santa

It is the night before Christmas, and Santa is on his way to bring presents to boys and girls all over the world. Here he is over Busytown. His first stop will be at Sergeant Murphy's house. Santa has some very nice toys for little Bridget Murphy.

CRASH!
Santa's sleigh lands too hard and
one of the runners breaks.
"What's all that noise up on my roof?"
asks a sleepy Sergeant Murphy.

Sergeant Murphy climbs on to the roof. He is very surprised to see Santa with his broken sleigh. "You're in real trouble now, Santa. I don't know how to repair your sleigh, but I will get Mr Fixit."

Sergeant Murphy jumps on his motorcycle and hurries to Mr Fixit's house. He pounds on the door. A sleepy Mr Fixit comes out, and off they go to fix Santa's sleigh.

But Mr Fixit is still half asleep and clumsily breaks the other runner. Santa is furious! "Now look what you've done!" he shouts.

"What's all that noise about?" calls Big Hilda from her house. Sergeant Murphy tells her and she says, "I'll be right over!"

So Big Hilda ploughs through the snow, carrying her skis.

"Here, Santa," she says. "You can fix your sleigh with these skis."

Mr Fixit offers to nail the skis to the sleigh. "No, thanks!" says Santa. "I will do it myself."

Now Santa can deliver the rest of his presents.

And what do you suppose Big Hilda finds in her stocking on Christmas morning? A NEW PAIR OF SKIS!

The Best Christmas Present Ever

On Christmas Eve, Pickles and Penny Pig hang up their stockings by the fireplace. It is cosy inside, but outside it is snowing hard. "I do hope this blizzard won't keep Santa from visiting us," says Penny.

They leave a plate of cookies and a cup of hot chocolate for Santa.

Then off to bed they go to dream about what Santa will bring them.

Daddy, Mummy and Aunt Rose stay up. Aunt Rose has come to visit for a few days, and they have a lot of things to talk about.

Later, Daddy puts on his cap and coat and goes out to the garage.

He shovels a path through the deep snow to the street. Now, why is he doing that at this time of night?

Look! Mummy is in the car with Daddy. They must be crazy to go for a ride on such a snowy night.

Uh, oh! They are stuck in a snowdrift! But a tow truck with a snow-plough comes to their rescue.

In the morning Pickles and Penny rush in
to see what Santa has brought them.

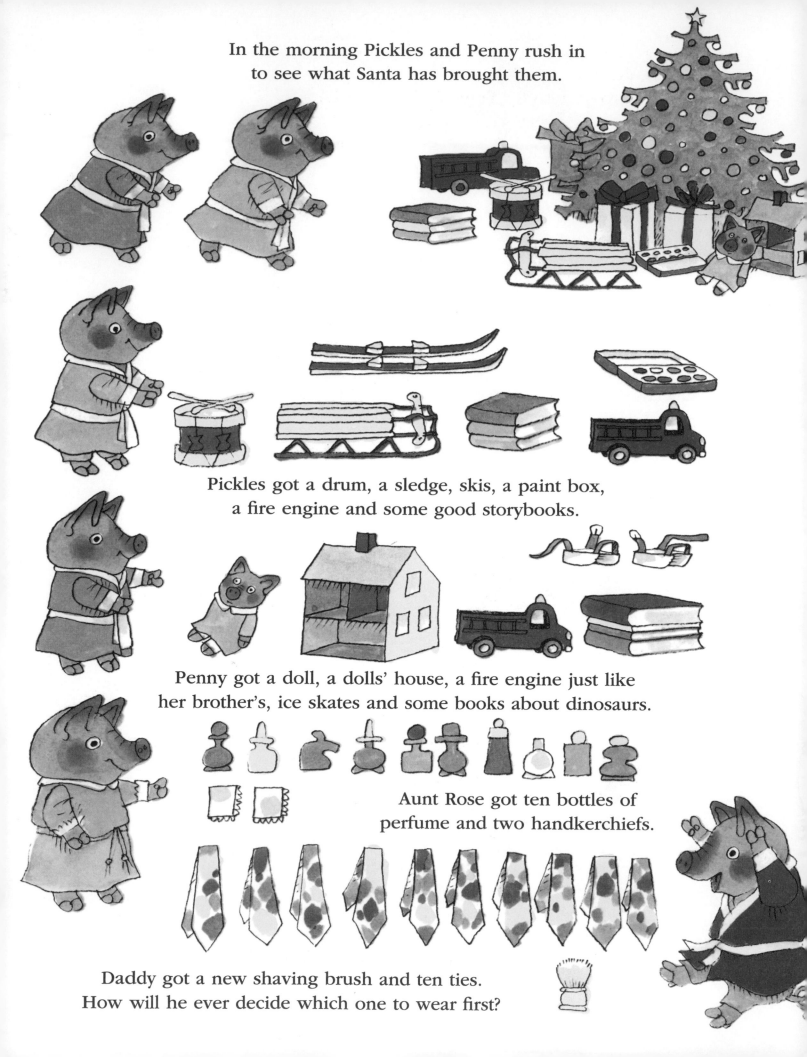

Pickles got a drum, a sledge, skis, a paint box,
a fire engine and some good storybooks.

Penny got a doll, a dolls' house, a fire engine just like
her brother's, ice skates and some books about dinosaurs.

Aunt Rose got ten bottles of
perfume and two handkerchiefs.

Daddy got a new shaving brush and ten ties.
How will he ever decide which one to wear first?

Then Pickles and Penny ask about Mummy.
What did SHE get? And where IS she?
"Mummy had to go into town last night to get her
present. It is a very special Christmas present," says
Daddy, who is as happy as can be. "Get your hats
and coats and let's go and see what she got."

They drive into town and stop at the Busytown Hospital.
Guess who they see inside the hospital?

There is Mummy with a little newborn baby
called Nicholas. Now, isn't that the best
Christmas present ever for the whole family?

Mr Frumble Helps Out

Who is that dressed like Santa?
Why, it is Mr Frumble! He is
invited to the Cat family's house
for Christmas dinner, and he wants
to thank them in his own special way.

Huckle, Sally and Lowly
are playing by the fireplace.
Suddenly they hear a noise.
Then some black soot falls
from the chimney. Can
Santa be coming again?

"Help! I'm stuck!" cries a voice. It is coming from
the chimney. Father Cat jumps up and rushes to the
fireplace. He reaches up the chimney and they all
help to pull. Out pops a very sooty Mr Frumble!
"Merry Christmas! Ho! Ho! Ho!" says Santa Frumble.

First he brushes the dirty soot off his suit.
It falls on the nice clean rug. Then he offers
to help with the dinner. He runs toward the
kitchen – and right into the Christmas tree!

CRASH! The tree falls over and Huckle and
Lowly have to set it back up again.

Mr Frumble decides to bake
a cake, but he spills the mixture
all over the floor.

The potatoes he is
cooking explode all
over the kitchen.

And the turkey he is roasting
gets burned. Smoke pours all
over the house, and firefighters
have to be called in.

"Thank you, Mr Frumble, but I really don't need your help," says Mother Cat.

"I'll just mop up this water," says Mr Frumble.
He swings the mop so hard that he breaks a table leg.
Everything crashes to the floor. Mother Cat will never
finish making the dinner with him around!

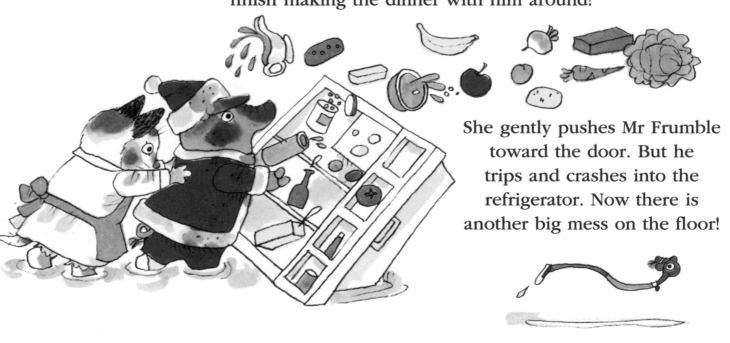

She gently pushes Mr Frumble
toward the door. But he
trips and crashes into the
refrigerator. Now there is
another big mess on the floor!

At last Mother Cat is alone in her kitchen. She
cleans up everything and then makes a wonderful
Christmas dinner. The children carry the food to
the table. She won't let Mr Frumble carry anything!

Mmmm! The dinner is delicious and everyone enjoys it – until butterfingers Mr Frumble drops the gravy boat and knocks over a big jug of grape juice. Now Mother Cat's beautiful tablecloth is bright purple.

Now it is time for dessert. And Mr Frumble has a very special dessert surprise for the Cat family and their guests. It is a HUGE cherry pie. He goes to the kitchen to get it.

Here he comes now. Just look at the size of that pie! It is so big that Mr Frumble has to balance it on his head. My, it is going to taste good! He walks very slowly and very carefully. Uh, oh, watch your step, Mr Frumble, there is a toy on the floor. Ohhh, no…

You guessed it!
Well, this is certainly the messiest Merry
Christmas ever. But everyone seems to be
having a *cherry* good time!

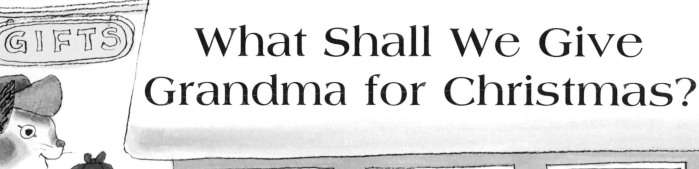

What Shall We Give Grandma for Christmas?

Huckle, Sally and Mother Cat want to get Grandma a nice Christmas present, but everything costs too much or is the wrong colour or size. Then they see Lowly, and he tells them how to MAKE the best Christmas present ever for Grandma and Grandpa or ANYONE. It is a pomander, and here is how you can make it:

Get a nice big apple and a jar of cloves.

Stick the cloves into the apple until it is completely covered with cloves.

Then tie a pretty red ribbon around the apple, and you have a sweet-smelling pomander. Grandma can put it in her clothes drawer or wardrobe, and it will smell sweet and spicy for many Christmases.

A Visit to Grandma's House

On Christmas morning, Father Cat opens the front door and discovers that it has snowed very hard during the night.

"I hope we can get to Grandma's house today," he says.

He shovels a path in the deep snow from the garage to the street.
My, that's hard work!

The Cat family start on their way but run into a big snowdrift.
Now they are STUCK!

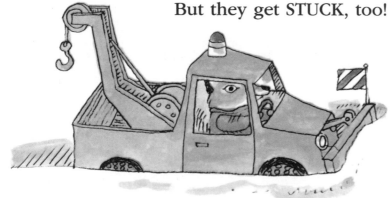

Farmer Pig and little Bugdozer come to pull them out.
But they get STUCK, too!

Mr Fixit comes in his tow truck. Guess what? He gets stuck. Now everyone is STUCK!

Along comes Lowly with his applecopter and sleigh.

And off they go to Grandma's house, singing "Jingle Bells" all the way.

Grandma is happy to see them. Look how pleased she is with her pomander apples! Now her clothes will smell lovely all year long. It's such a nice present… and from such nice grandchildren!

A Visit to Grandma's House Game

These are the rules for the game on the next two pages.

You will need four coins, and a small square of cardboard for each player, with his or her initials on it. Ask a grown-up to cut them out and help you initial them.

1. *Who goes first?* Each player tosses the four coins. The player with the most "heads" goes first, the one with the next most goes second, and so on. Each player starts with his or her "piece" (the square of cardboard) at the Cat family's house.

2. *How to move.* When it's your turn, toss the four coins. The number of heads you get is the number of spaces you should move your piece along the road to Grandma's house.

If you land on a space with another player's piece on it already, you lose your next turn.

3. *Rewards and penalties.* When you land on a reward or penalty space, do what it says.

4. *Who wins?* The first player to reach Grandma's house wins the game. He or she gets a kiss from Grandma.

NO MOVE ALLOWED

MOVE 1 SPACE

MOVE 2 SPACES

MOVE 3 SPACES

MOVE 4 SPACES

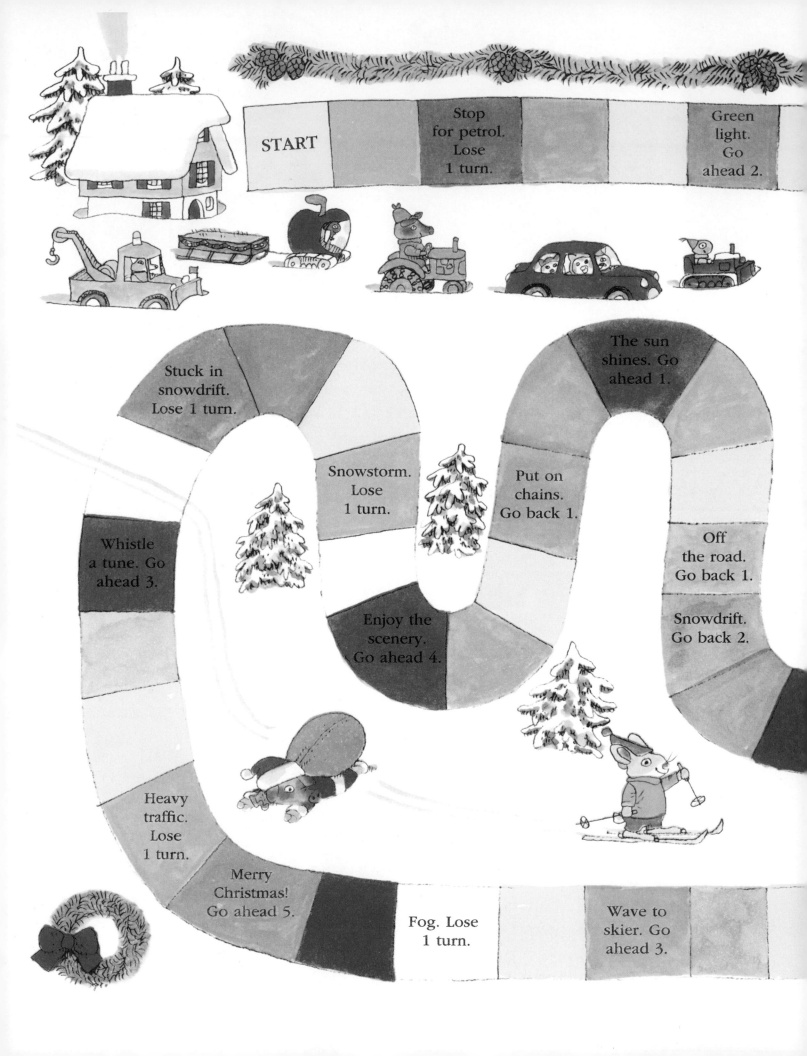

START

Stop for petrol. Lose 1 turn.

Green light. Go ahead 2.

Stuck in snowdrift. Lose 1 turn.

Snowstorm. Lose 1 turn.

Put on chains. Go back 1.

The sun shines. Go ahead 1.

Whistle a tune. Go ahead 3.

Enjoy the scenery. Go ahead 4.

Off the road. Go back 1.

Snowdrift. Go back 2.

Heavy traffic. Lose 1 turn.

Merry Christmas! Go ahead 5.

Fog. Lose 1 turn.

Wave to skier. Go ahead 3.

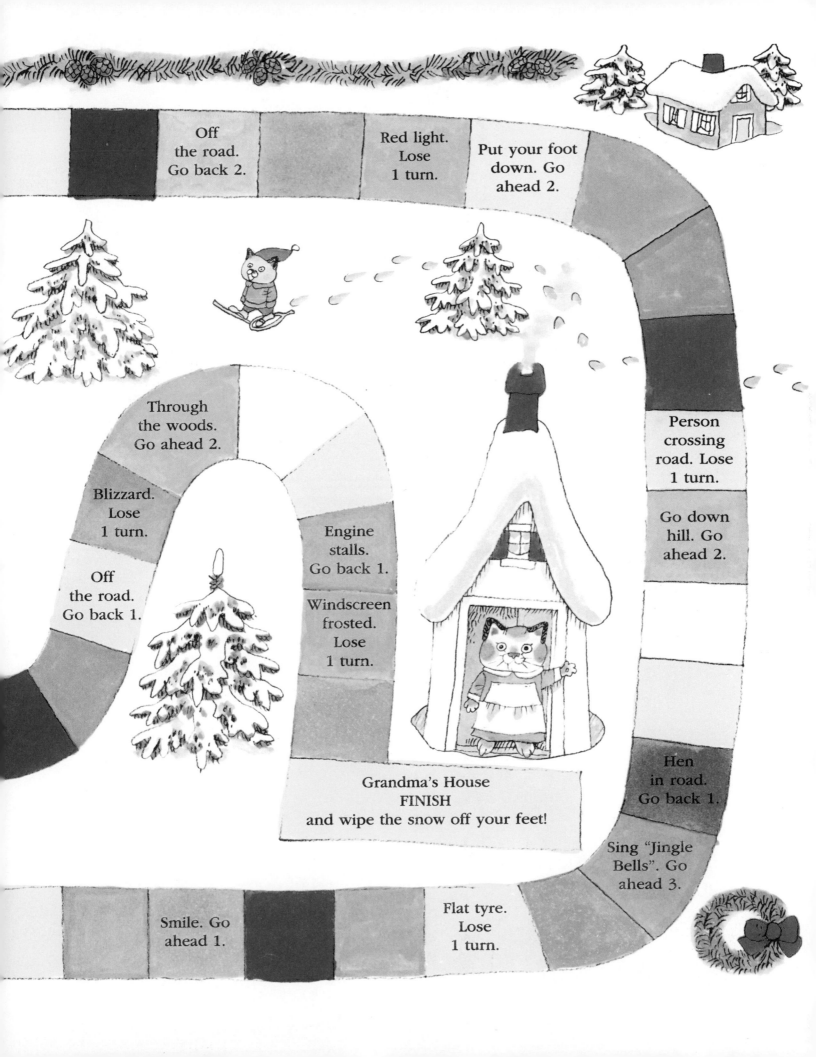

Off the road. Go back 2.

Red light. Lose 1 turn.

Put your foot down. Go ahead 2.

Through the woods. Go ahead 2.

Blizzard. Lose 1 turn.

Off the road. Go back 1.

Engine stalls. Go back 1.

Windscreen frosted. Lose 1 turn.

Person crossing road. Lose 1 turn.

Go down hill. Go ahead 2.

Grandma's House
FINISH
and wipe the snow off your feet!

Hen in road. Go back 1.

Sing "Jingle Bells". Go ahead 3.

Smile. Go ahead 1.

Flat tyre. Lose 1 turn.

The Naughty Twins

Once there were twins named Abe and Babe who were so naughty that everyone called them "double trouble." They were really horrible!

They liked to argue and fight and push people in the mud.

They always shouted and interrupted other people.

They thought it was fun to break things that didn't belong to them.

At the playground they took toys away from little children.

They ate with their fingers and made a mess of everything. Their table manners were terrible! Even their mother had to agree that if there was anything bad, rude or nasty that could be done, they would do it.

Santa does not bring nice presents to naughty boys and girls. Instead, he fills their stockings with dirty lumps of coal.

So on Christmas morning Abe and Babe got a big surprise. Two HUGE sacks of coal were all that Santa brought them. That's how naughty they were!

Abe and Babe were very sad. They knew that Santa was punishing them for being so naughty. "We must learn to be good," they said to each other.

Outside, everyone was playing with their new sledges. Abe and Babe watched them sadly.

"I wish we had a sledge," said Abe.

"And I wish we had some electricity," said Sergeant Murphy. "The snowstorm broke the electrical lines, and without electricity there are going to be a lot of cold houses and uncooked Christmas dinners."

Abe and Babe felt sorry for all the people whose Christmas day would be spoiled. "This is our chance to be good," Abe said to Babe. They told Sergeant Murphy their plan. "That's a splendid idea!" he said.

Sergeant Murphy called the children together and told them to take their sledges to the twins' house.

"Not on your life!" said the children. "Those twins are double trouble." But Sergeant Murphy assured them that everything would be all right.

When the children got to the twins' house, Abe and Babe dragged their big sacks of coal outside. Then they filled a paper bag with coal for each child.

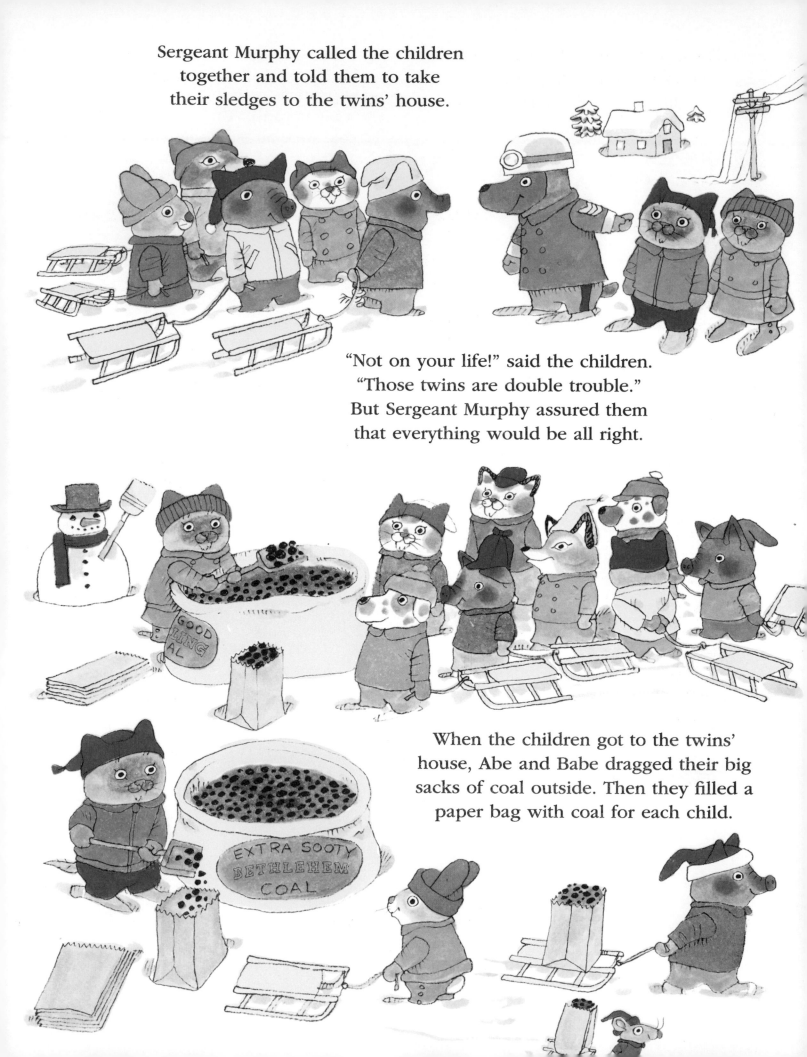

The children gave the coal to their families to burn on their barbecues.
That Christmas all the dinners in Busytown were cooked on barbecues!
The dinners were delicious!

Santa always leaves a few extra toys at the fire station to give to children he might have missed. So when Santa heard about Abe and Babe's good deed, he called the fire chief right away and told him to see that Abe and Babe got some really nice Christmas presents.

From that day on, the naughty twins became good twins. And every Christmas after that, the twins received a tiny piece of coal in their stockings to remind them of their good deed on that cold Christmas day.

Christmas Words

Chimney

Star

Wreath

Candle

Ornaments

Cards

Stockings

Dining room table

Tree

Fireplace

Christmas presents

Kitchen

Mummy cooking

Pie

Cookies

Turkey

Snowball

Carol singers

Snowman

Church

Snow

Bell

Daddy's new tie

Mistletoe

Sledge

Skis

Saucer sledge

Snow fort

Skates

Ice

Hockey stick

Mr Frumble Santa Claus

Sack

Skating rink

Footprints in the snow

Silent Night

Joseph Mohr   Franz Gruber

2.
Silent night, holy night!
Shepherds quake at the sight;
Glories stream from heaven afar,
Heavenly hosts sing *Alleluia*,
Christ the Saviour is born!
Christ the Saviour is born!

3.
Silent night, holy night!
Son of God, love's pure light
Radiant beams from Thy holy face,
With the dawn of redeeming grace,
Jesus, Lord, at Thy Birth,
Jesus, Lord, at Thy Birth.